His friends ran out into Watling Street, shrieking and pretending to be afraid. As Sam dived after them, he spotted some of the French boys from Cheapside.

"Get the frogs!" he shouted.

There were three French boys. Sam and his friends often scrapped with them, jeering at their funny clothes and strange frog language.

At once a fight began. Two of the French boys gave as good as they got. The third was slight and clever-looking, but not tough. He also had a limp.

Sam's master was a shoemaker and Sam had sometimes seen this boy in the shop. He needed special shoes.

"Gammy-leg frog – hop back to France!"
Sam shouted.

The boy turned and faced him. "I was
born in London, stupid," he said.

There was a superior air about him that
annoyed Sam.

"You're a frog! Hop along, frog – you
can't even walk properly!"

Sam gave him a shove. The boy
stumbled and fell sprawling in a pile of
horse muck. Sam and his friends hooted
with laughter as their victim struggled to
get up, then tried furiously to wipe the
mess from his sleeves and breeches.

Sam knew he was in the wrong, but

he didn't care. He didn't like the French boy, anyway.

As the fight rolled on, a brewer's cart appeared, forcing a path through the crowded street. The two groups scattered, and the French boys disappeared.

Sam knew he'd be expected back at his master's shop. He ran off towards Friday Street.

* * *

The dog, Budge, was sunning himself on the shoemaker's doorstep. He saw Sam and got up to be fussed. His tail thumped

Sam's leg. He was a small, scruffy mongrel with a bitten ear.

"Come on, Budge," said Sam. "Dinner." He felt hungry.

There was a smell of cooking inside. Alice, their maid, was stirring stew in a large pot that hung over the fire and talking to William Kemp, Sam's master.

"Five hundred across London dead of plague last week! And it's taken hold in this parish now."

Sam knew she must have been to Cheapside and seen the latest Bill of Mortality – the list of the dead that was put up once a week.

"Hallo, Sam!" she said. "Give those scraps to Budge, will you?"

As soon as Sam put Budge's meat down for him the dog began gobbling eagerly, his nose pushing against Sam's hand. Behind him, Sam heard his master say, "That's bad news. We'll have to pinch and scrape to get by. Most of my best customers have left the city already."

Sam stood up. "Will we leave, Master?"

William Kemp laughed. "I wish we could! But I'm old. I've no family, and no one to go to outside London. You're my only family, Sam."

Master Kemp had taken Sam from

the orphanage two years ago, when Sam was about seven, to work as a servant and perhaps, when he was older, to become his apprentice. Sam remembered how happy he had been to leave the orphanage. Master Kemp was kind to him, and Alice fed him well and looked after them both. Of course, William Kemp beat Sam when he was lazy or at fault, but he didn't starve or overwork him the way some masters did. Sam had always wanted a family. Now he had Master Kemp and Alice – and Budge.

Alice cut hunks of bread and ladled stew into bowls. "My mother says she wishes I was home. She's afraid for me."

Alice's mother lived across the river, at Southwark.

"You won't leave us, will you?" asked Sam in alarm.

"Of course not, silly!" Alice ruffled his hair. "I like earning my own living here. Besides, there are four younger ones back home to feed and clothe, so my money helps." She smiled – a small, tight smile.

"We'll get through this together," William Kemp assured them both. "I've lived through times of plague before. It'll come to an end when the cold weather arrives, and we'll all survive, God willing."

All Cats and Dogs

The next day Sam was running an errand in Cheapside when the town crier appeared and began ringing a bell.

"...all cats and dogs," Sam heard as he drew closer. "Carts will be sent around the streets. Drivers will be paid a bounty of two pennies for every corpse brought in. All cats and dogs to be killed! Diseased animals carry the plague as they run about the city..."

Budge isn't diseased! thought Sam. *He has a few fleas, but don't we all? And he doesn't run about – well… not much. He guards the shop, and he sits in the sun. And I love him. They can't kill Budge!*

He ran home to tell his master and Alice.

"Don't worry. We'll keep him in," said William Kemp. "They don't have the right to search people's houses."

But Budge didn't want to be kept in. The doorstep was his favourite place. He liked to sit there and watch all the life of the busy street. Inside, he barked and whined and scrabbled at the door.

A few days later a cart came down

the street and they heard the squeals of animals cornered and clubbed to death. The men joked as they tossed the corpses into their cart.

"Ugh! That's horrible!" exclaimed Alice. "Come away from the window, Sam."

"Tuppence a corpse – you can't blame them," said William Kemp.

But they don't have to enjoy it, Sam thought.

It was impossible to ignore the danger now, with Budge hidden indoors, and news that the King and all his people had moved out of London to Hampton Court to escape the pestilence.

"There's a man in Bread Street selling medicine," said Alice. "He says it'll keep you safe from plague. People were queuing up to buy it."

"What's in it?" asked William Kemp.

"Some secret remedy from the East, he says."

"Rubbish!" scoffed Master Kemp.

But later that day he sent Alice to buy a bottle of it, just in case.

He drank some himself and gave a spoonful to Sam. The cloudy green liquid tasted disgusting. It made Sam feel sick. But Master Kemp said they should all take some every day.

Alice also bought posies of herbs from a woman in the market. She gave one to Sam.

"Hold it close to your nose and mouth when you go out," she said, a serious look in her eyes. "It'll protect you from infected air."

"And walk near the middle of the road," William Kemp added. "Don't get too close to other people."

Everyone took precautions. But the next week, when the weather was hotter than ever, they heard that Sam's friend John Jenks had died of plague. Sam saw his friend's body, tied in a shroud, put on a cart with a heap of others and taken away – no coffin, no bearers to carry him to the churchyard.

The house where John had lived was shut up and the door padlocked. A red cross was painted on the door and, next to it, the words, 'Lord have mercy upon us'. No one would be allowed out until forty days after the last person inside had either died or been found to be free of plague.

Sam could hardly believe that just two weeks ago he and John had been playing together in the streets. The plague had seemed a fun game then. Now it was a terrifying reality.

3

Death All Around

"Oh! Those bells! They drive me mad!"
Alice exclaimed.

The church bells rang almost all the
time now, to mark the passing of those who
had died. Day and night you could hear the
plague carts rumbling over the cobbles, the
cry of, "Bring out your dead!" and the thump
of bodies being flung into the carts.

Despite the bells, Alice was cheerful,

humming a tune as she went about her work. Sam knew it was because tomorrow was her day off. She would be going home to Southwark to see her mother and sisters.

"You can strip your own bed, Sam, since you're up here," she said.

They were in Master Kemp's bedchamber and Alice was changing the sheets.

Sam slept on a low bed in one corner of the room. He hardly needed sheets at all, he thought, the weather was so hot. It was mid-August, a month since they had started keeping Budge indoors. In the heat of the midday sun, the upper floor of the house felt like a furnace.

"It's so hot," Sam sighed. "Shall I open the window? The bells have stopped now."

"Don't you dare!" said Alice. "You know the fishmonger across the way died yesterday. The rest of them are boarded up inside."

Sam saw that the fishmonger's upstairs windows were open – and the upper floors of their two houses were only yards apart.

"If you stood here and breathed in, you could catch the pestilence from their house," Alice went on. "It shouldn't be allowed."

"What shouldn't?" asked Sam, confused.

"People in plague houses having their upstairs windows open!" snapped Alice.

"Have you done that bed yet?"

"Yes," said Sam. Before she could find another job for him, he added, "I'll go and feed Budge now."

Downstairs, Master Kemp was busy tidying his workshop. "Just getting ready for when my customers return," he said.

Budge was fretting at the back door. Sam let the dog out, to a patch of earth in the yard. But he dared not allow him to stay outside for long.

The yard stank. And over everything, in the air, was a rotten, putrid smell – the smell of corpses.

Later in the morning William Kemp said to Sam, "Church today."

"Must we go?"

"We must. You know that."

The Lord Mayor had ordered every Wednesday to be a day of prayer and fasting, and everyone had to attend church.

"It's that churchyard," Sam said. "I hate it now."

The path to the entrance of St Matthew's church led between newly filled graves. There were so many that the dead were heaped up either side of the path, one on top of another. The stench was overpowering. Even inside the church the sickening smell lingered, despite the flowers and herbs placed all around. The bell tolled dolefully.

When Sam saw all the people on their knees and heard the prayers and weeping, he felt sure that God would listen to them. Somehow he couldn't believe he would die, like poor John Jenks or the fishmonger.

The congregation was reciting the ninety-first Psalm: "He is my refuge and my fortress: my God; in him will I trust... Thou shalt not be afraid for the terror by night... nor for the pestilence that walketh in darkness..."

Alice said afterwards, "I like those words. They comfort me."

But in the evening, William Kemp sighed and said he felt uncommonly tired.

"I'll take an extra dose of that medicine," he said. "A night's rest will put me right."

4

The Apothecary

Sam was woken early next morning by the sound of William Kemp tossing and sighing.

He got up and peeped between the bed-curtains. "Master? Are you unwell?"

William Kemp's eyes were glassy, his face flushed.

Sam began to tremble. His insides felt hollow. He ran across the landing and knocked on the door of Alice's room.

She opened it, dressed in her best yellow gown.

"I'm off to my mother's," she said. "What's the matter, Sam?"

"Master Kemp is ill."

"Oh! Don't worry. He often has these turns." She smiled.

"No – he's feverish. Please come and look at him!"

Sam could see she wanted to be on her way, but she followed him into the room. It had an unhealthy smell. William Kemp groaned, and said, "Alice, send Sam for the apothecary. I fear it may be the plague."

"Don't say that, Master!" Alice protested.

"It'll be some chill you picked up in church yesterday." But Sam saw that her face had gone white and she stood well back from the bed.

She led Sam outside. "You heard what your master said? Go now, and fetch the apothecary. He will know how to cool the fever, and he'll give Master Kemp some medicine. I'll see you later, when I get back from Southwark."

Sam clung to her, tears stinging his eyes. "Don't go! Wait till the apothecary has been!"

"I can't, Sam," said Alice. She pulled herself out of Sam's grasp. "My mother's expecting me."

"Please!" he begged. "Please, Alice – stay!"

But she was already on her way downstairs. "Goodbye, Sam!" she cried, her voice sounding higher than usual, and he heard the door open, then close firmly behind her.

* * *

The apothecary lived on Bread Street. Sam lifted the latch and crept inside the shop, into a dim cluttered space that smelt of herbs and spices. There were scales and measuring spoons, and rows of bottles and small earthenware pots. Behind the counter the apothecary, Master Burton, was mixing something in a bowl. Sam knew he made nearly all the remedies himself.

"Excuse me, sir," said Sam. "My master sent me. He's sick, with a fever."

"I'll come at once," said Master Burton.

He gathered some medicines and instruments. Then he went into the back room and came out wearing a long black, waxed cloak and carrying a white stick and a strange leather helmet with a long beak.

"You've seen a helmet like this before, haven't you, Sam?"

Sam nodded. The sight of it made him feel sick with fear.

"It's nothing to be frightened of," Master Burton said. "I can see through these eye-pieces – they are made of horn – and the beak is stuffed with herbs to protect me from infected air." He put it on. "You see?"

3

Inside the helmet his voice sounded muffled and strange.

They set off together along the street, the terrifying beaked figure stalking along beside Sam like a giant bird of prey.

Budge began to bark at the beaked stranger as soon as they entered William Kemp's house.

"Ssh! He's here to help," said Sam, and he shut Budge into the storeroom and led Master Burton upstairs.

"Heat some water, will you?" the apothecary said, as he went into William Kemp's room. "I may need to make poultices."

It was not long before he came back down to the kitchen, where Sam was heating a kettle over the fire. "I'm sorry, Sam. Your master has the plague. I found swellings under his arms and on his neck."

He wrung out two cloths in the hot water and smeared them with a strong-smelling paste made of herbs. He left the pot of paste on the table.

"I will lay these poultices on the swellings to draw the poison out," he said. "When the cloths cool, make some more."

He also gave Sam a bottle of medicine. "Give your master a spoonful of this twice a day."

"Will it cure him?" Sam asked. He wished he could see the man's face.

"It may, if God wills it," came the apothecary's muffled reply.

Sam went to Master Kemp's pot of coins in the workshop. He counted out the money to pay the apothecary, dropping the coins into a dish of vinegar on the counter to disinfect them.

"You know I must notify the authorities?" Master Burton said.

Sam nodded. His lower lip trembled. "They'll lock us in, won't they?"

"Yes. I'm sorry."

"What about Alice, our maid? She won't be back till evening. "

Master Burton hesitated. "They'll let

her back in... if she asks." He put a hand on Sam's shoulder. "God be with you, Sam."

Soon after Master Burton left, two men came to shut up the house. They worked quickly, nailing closed the downstairs windows and the back door.

"Stop!" Sam protested. "Our maid will be back later!" He was trembling. They were going to leave him alone with his sick master. What if Master Kemp got worse? What if he died?

"We can't wait. It's not allowed," one of them said. "You'll have a watchman outside, day and night, and he'll look after you. Do you have a basket, and some twine?"

Sam nodded.

"Tie it to your upper window frame and let it down when you need to bring anything in."

The men shut the shop door behind them as they left, and then Sam heard banging and hammering and the rattle of a chain. He was seized with sudden terror. "No! No!" he screamed. "Let me out! Please!" He beat on the door with his fists. He heaved at it, but it would not open. How would Alice ever get back in? By now the men would be marking the door with the dreaded cross and the words, 'Lord have mercy upon us'. He shouted and hammered on it with his fists until they were bruised. Then, not knowing what else to do, he sank down on the floor and cried.

Through his tears he heard a distant barking and scrabbling. Budge! He ran to let the dog out of the storeroom. Budge jumped up at him and wagged his tail.

"Oh, Budge!" said Sam. He hugged the dog and buried his face in his fur.

 **5**

Locked In

For the rest of that day William Kemp burned with a fever. Sam gave him sips of beer and made new hot poultices.

Even Budge seemed to know that something was wrong. He lay on his master's bed and guarded him, as if from an invisible enemy.

Sam longed for Alice to come back. "Where is she?" he asked Budge, stroking the dog's ears for comfort. "Master Kemp is getting worse, and I don't know what to do."

Outside, a rough-looking watchman was sitting in the street, a jug of beer at his side. This man would fetch anything Sam needed – food, or medicine. But it was Alice, with her friendly chatter and practical ways, that Sam really wanted.

A howl from the bed made him rush to his master's side. William Kemp was clawing at his clothes.

"The pain!" he gasped. "I can't bear it!"

He struggled out of bed and hurled himself around the room, banging his head against the walls.

"Master! Get back into bed!" begged Sam. "You'll hurt yourself."

He struggled to restrain the sick man.

"Please!" Sam felt desperate.

At last he got William Kemp to lie down again. As he untied the neck of his master's night-shirt to help cool him, Sam saw to his horror that there was a purple rash across the man's chest. The tokens! He knew that once the tokens appeared, the sufferer did not have long to live.

Sam began to tremble. "Oh, Budge!" he cried. "Where is Alice? She should be home by now."

He ran to the window.

"Watchman!" he called. "Have you seen our maid – Alice?"

The man shrugged.

"She was wearing a yellow gown."

"Ah! Young woman, slim?"

"Yes!" said Sam.

"She came by, not long ago. I saw her staring up at your window. She was crying. At least, that's what it looked like. Asked her if she wanted anything, but she said no, she was on her way home. And off she went – double quick."

"But – I need to see her – to tell her..."

"You won't see her again, I reckon."

She can't have left us! Sam thought.

He turned away from the window, and his voice shook as he said, "Master – Alice has left us! She's gone!"

William Kemp struggled to speak. "Don't blame her... Sam. Only a saint would come back in. The cross... on the door..."

"But she didn't even say goodbye!" Sam wailed, unable to hold back his tears.

"Give me some medicine now," said Master Kemp. "Then I'll sleep and let you rest."

* * *

The next morning, when Sam went to check on Master Kemp, Budge growled at him. Sam saw, with a shock, that his master was dead. William Kemp lay with his eyes open, staring at nothing.

Sam murmured a prayer for his good master's soul. For a long time he sat on the bed next to Budge, feeling lonely and sorrowful, knowing he should tell someone what had happened. Budge was warm, but William Kemp grew cold.

At last Sam called the watchman.

"The cart will come by around midday," the man said. "Be ready with the corpse."

Sam shuddered. He thought, I must make a shroud. And again he longed for Alice's help.

He used the bed sheet under William Kemp's body. Budge growled and bared his teeth. He didn't want anyone to touch his dead master. "Come on, Budge, please," said Sam, as he moved the dog off the bed. "I don't want to do this, but I must." Carefully, he covered the body and tied the two ends of the sheet at the top and the bottom. As soon as he was done, Budge jumped back up and lay down against the shrouded figure.

Later, Sam heard cartwheels crashing over the cobbles.

"Bring out your dead!" a weary voice called.

Sam leaned out of the window and saw the cart already piled high with corpses.

"I can't lift him!" he shouted.

He heard someone at the door, opening the padlock. Budge's ears pricked up.

Two burly men came up the stairs, into the bedchamber. Budge stood guard over William Kemp's body, growling fiercely. One of the men hit him and he yelped in pain.

"Don't!" Sam sprang forward to protect his dog.

"Hold onto him, then!"

Sam obeyed, and the two men grabbed the body and carried it down the stairs and out of the door. They tossed it into the cart along with the rest of the corpses.

Tears ran down Sam's face. Shutting Budge in the bedchamber, he hurried downstairs shouting, "Wait! Can I go with you to the churchyard?"

One of the men laughed. "Churchyard! The churchyard's full. We're going to the pit in Moorfields. You don't want to go there, son."

"I do! I want —"

The door banged shut in his face.

"Forty days!" the men shouted, as the watchman locked Sam up again in the house. "And keep that dog in or the bounty men will get him."

Forty days. Sam sat on the stairs. He had never felt more alone in his life. Forty days — and then, if he was still alive, what would they do with him? He'd end up back at the orphanage — or, more likely, at the Bridewell, which was little better than a prison.

One thing was certain. Wherever they sent him, they wouldn't let him keep Budge. And Budge was all he had left.

6

Escape

"Basket for you!"

Sam leaned out, and saw the watchman putting meat and a jug of beer into the basket. Carefully, he hauled it up. Budge watched, pacing about and wagging his tail. He knew the basket meant food for him, too.

The air outside was full of smoke from the bonfires burning to drive away the pestilence.

Sam noticed something else. "The bells

have stopped ringing!" he called to the watchman.

"Lord Mayor's orders! Good thing, too!"

Sam fed Budge some scraps of meat. "This is day eighteen," he told the dog with a sigh. "Only another twenty-two days to go."

Since William Kemp's death he had been marking the days on the kitchen wall. By now he felt sure he had not caught the plague.

He went into his master's deserted workshop and looked around. Pieces of shaped brown leather lay on the table, ready for stitching. On the shelves above were several pairs of finished shoes whose owners had never called for them. There were balls of twine, awls and needles. None of it needed any more.

Like me, thought Sam. *I'm not needed either. When my forty days are up they will let us out, send me away – and kill Budge. We have to escape!*

But how? All the downstairs windows were nailed shut. Upstairs, the window in William Kemp's bedchamber overlooked the street, and the watchman sat below day and night. It would have to be the window in the little back room where Alice had slept.

The problem was Budge.

"I can't go without you," he told the dog. "But you mustn't bark. And how am I going to get you down?"

An idea came to him. The basket!

That night Sam made himself stay awake till he had heard the dead-cart pass and the streets were deserted and quiet.

The basket, he reckoned, was just about big enough to hold Budge. He left it in the back bedchamber and went downstairs. He took a handful of coins from William Kemp's workshop and put them in a purse that he hid under his clothes. In the kitchen he found bread and cheese for himself and a meaty bone for Budge. He wrapped the food in a cloth and filled a leather flask with beer.

"Come on, Budge!" he whispered.

Budge could smell the meat, and whined

hopefully, wagging his tail, as he followed
Sam upstairs. Sam tied the end of the rope
to Alice's bed frame. He opened the window.
But as soon as he tried to persuade Budge
to get into the basket the dog began to bark.
The sound shattered the silence.

"No, Budge! No! Bad dog!" whispered Sam.

Should I muzzle him with twine? he
wondered.

But the stern words had worked – for now.

Sam grabbed the dog quickly, lifted him
into the basket, and tied the handles together.
Before Budge could escape he heaved the
basket up onto the sill and began to lower it
into the yard.

Budge was alarmed, and whined pitifully. As soon as he was down he sprang out and began barking again.

"Budge!" called Sam. "Here!" He tossed him the bone. At once there was a contented silence.

Sam grasped the rope and lowered himself over the sill. He slithered fast, skinning his hands, and dropped down beside Budge.

He listened. All was quiet.

He pulled Budge's lead from his pocket and fastened it to the dog's collar. As they set off he took great gulps of the night air.

They were free!

7

Alone in the City

Sam and Budge scurried as fast as
they could away from Friday Street. The
watchman would report their escape in the
morning, and they needed to hide.

They crossed Cheapside and entered a
tangle of streets and alleys on the north side.
Sam felt scared. He didn't know this area at
all. He kept walking until he was too tired to
go any further, then sat down on a doorstep.

"We'll eat our food and rest here till morning," he said to Budge, cuddling up to the dog to stay warm.

At first light he heard doors opening, voices, and a clatter of pails. Quickly, he gathered his possessions and led Budge away.

Further along the street, grass was growing between the cobblestones. Sam saw two houses with the red cross on them, and one with the white cross that meant the house was now clear of infection. Many shops were shuttered and empty. At the back of one of them he noticed a shed surrounded by tall weeds.

"Perhaps we could hide there," he said, leading Budge into the yard. He pulled aside some of the weeds and tried the door of the shed. It opened. There was a smell of wood shavings and straw. Some broken chairs were piled at the back. In one corner was a heap of old sacks.

"A bed!" sighed Sam.

It was what he'd been longing for all night. He curled up on the sacks with Budge beside him and fell into a deep sleep.

When Sam awoke, he felt hungry. He'd need to buy food – but he couldn't take Budge.

"I don't like leaving you," he said, as he tied Budge to a fence post in the yard.

Budge didn't like it either. He looked so mournful that Sam nearly changed his mind.

But Budge would be worth two pennies dead. Sam couldn't risk losing him as well.

In the next street he found a butcher's shop and bought a meat pie that was big enough for him and Budge to share.

As he fed Budge the scraps back at the shed, Sam looked at the coins he'd brought and worked out how long the two of them could last on a pie a day, and beer. At least a week, he reckoned. That seemed a long time.

Sam and Budge spent two more days in their hiding-place. No one came into the yard. Each day Sam bought a pie from the butcher. Gradually he began to feel safe. But on the third day, as he left the shop, he saw a gang of boys watching him with a mean look in their eyes. Alarmed, he ran off quickly, taking a path that led away from Budge and the shed.

The gang followed him.

Like a pack of wolves they circled round, one barring his way at every turn, others nipping in and jostling him.

"Leave me alone!" Sam shoved his way out, and ran, his heart thudding, towards a busier street. When he dared look back he saw, to his relief, that they were going away.

He was shaking when at last he found his way back to the empty house and crept into the shed. Budge licked him, and he stroked the dog and felt calmer. But later, when he reached for the purse he had hidden under his clothes, he found that it was gone. The boys had stolen it.

Now he would have to beg.

8

Caught!

"Oi! Be off with you!" The baker
stormed out of his shop and glared at Sam.
"You're driving my customers away."

Sam moved further up the street. He
hoped people coming out of the shops
would take pity on him. He was very
hungry. Yesterday a maidservant had
given him some stale bread, but he'd eaten
nothing since. People hurried by, clutching

their posies of herbs to their faces. No one took any notice of him.

He was searching for scraps among the cobblestones when a woman came by and gave him a bun.

"Thank you –" he began. But she was already gone – afraid of catching the plague.

The bun was warm and fresh and flavoured with cinnamon. He devoured it ravenously. Nothing, he thought, had ever tasted so good.

He licked the last of the crumbs from his fingers as he ran back to the shed to look for Budge.

"Oh, Budge, I'm sorry," he said, when he

saw his poor dog curled up on the ground. "I've nothing for you again."

Budge didn't even look up, and growled when Sam tried to stroke him. *He'll turn wild and leave me if I don't feed him,* Sam thought.

Things were getting desperate. He knew he must find help soon or they would both starve.

The next morning Budge barked and struggled as Sam tried to tie him up.

"You can't come, Budge," Sam told him. "They'll kill you for two pennies, and you're all I've got! I'll find you some food. I promise." He left his dog straining at the tether and whimpering.

In Foster Lane he passed a row of houses with shops at the front. It was early, and the shops were still closed, but at the end of one of the side passages he saw a half-open door. He ran towards the doorway, hoping to meet someone kind-hearted.

He knocked twice, but no one answered, so he pushed the door open cautiously and peered in. He could hear voices from somewhere in the house, but the room in front of him was empty except for a cat with a yellow stare. A fire was burning in the grate, and over it hung an iron pot that gave off the mouth-watering fragrance of meat and herbs. Sam's stomach yearned for the contents of that pot. On the table was a knife, a dish of butter and half a loaf of bread.

Sam didn't stop to think. Driven by hunger, he darted in, grabbed the loaf, turned – and found the doorway blocked by a tall girl with a yoke across her shoulders carrying two pails of water.

"Mother!" she shouted. "There's a thief!"

A woman burst into the kitchen from the inner door. Sam ran and tried to pass the girl, but the yoke and pails blocked his way. And then, to his horrified surprise, Budge came racing down the passage with his chewed lead trailing behind him, and shot into the house.

The cat stood up and hissed. Budge barked. Cat, Budge and Sam all moved at once. They collided in the middle of the room and Sam fell flat on the floor, dropping the bread as he smacked down onto the hard flagstones.

The woman seized him. She shook
him and shouted in a language he didn't
understand, and Sam cried out, "Sorry! I'm
sorry! Please, I'm so hungry..." while Budge
barked and the girl glared at Sam and said,
"Dirty little ragamuffin! We'll call the
constable –"

"Please –" Sam was almost crying now as
he reached out for the bread.

The woman stopped shaking him, and
looked him over with angry eyes. Then
something in her face softened.

"*Il a faim*," she said, "*voilà tout*." She
took a bowl from a shelf and went to the pot
over the fire.

Sam, watching her, thought: *I've seen her before.* But he couldn't think where.

She put the full bowl down on the table, set a spoon beside it, and picked up the loaf from the ground. She cut a thick slice, then gestured to Sam to sit down.

"Eat," she said. "Eat, and then we talk."

9

Changes

Sam gobbled the stew so fast it burned his mouth. Budge found the cat's bowl and swallowed its contents in one gulp.

A lot of talk in two languages was going on over Sam's head. More people had come into the room, but it was only when he had finished the last crumb of bread that he raised his head and looked at them all. Apart from the woman and the angry girl, there was a man, two younger girls – and a boy he recognised with a shock as the lame French boy he had bullied in Watling Street. And now he knew why the woman had looked so familiar. She used to bring the boy – her son – to the shoemaker's to be fitted.

The mother sent the children out, back into the inner room. She sounded anxious, and he caught the word "pestilence".

"I don't have the pestilence!" he said indignantly.

The man faced him. "You are sure?"

"Yes! My master –" The thought of Master Kemp and how happy he'd been at the shop in Friday Street brought a lump to Sam's throat; it was hard to talk. "My master died of it weeks ago. But I am well. Only... now I have nowhere to go."

"You have no family?"

Sam shook his head. "There was Alice, our maid. But she left us. Please – don't call the constables! They'll take me to the Bridewell. And then my dog..." He felt tears rising again.

"Don't be afraid," said the French woman gently. "Tell us how you came to be here."

And so Sam told them everything.

Afterwards, the woman cut another slice of bread and some cheese, and Sam wolfed it down while Budge was backed into a corner by the outraged cat. The adults talked together in French. Sam could tell that they were sad to hear of Master Kemp's death.

At last, the man turned to Sam and said, "You need a new home."

Sam nodded.

"Your master made shoes for our family. We liked him. He was always kind and patient with our son, who has suffered much because he is lame."

At this Sam felt ashamed, thinking of his own disgraceful behaviour towards the French boy.

"In return for your master's kindness, we want to help you," the man went on. "Now, we had a servant – a boy a little older than you. He left us in the spring. If you agree, we could take you in his place –"

"Oh, yes! Thank you!" cried Sam.

"It would be a trial period at first. We'd expect you to work hard –"

"I can work, sir! You'll be pleased with me, I promise!"

The man smiled. "Good. Then it is agreed. What is your name, boy?"

"Sam Maylam, sir."

"And I am Paul Giraud. I'm a jeweller and have my workshop here. This is my wife, and my daughter, Thérèse. Also you saw my son, André, and the little girls."

"Thank you, sir," said Sam again and again.

He felt a huge sense of relief and gratitude. But he also felt anxious about André, the man's son. He knew that, as a servant, he would be under André's control, and he was sure the French boy would find ways of taking revenge. But the thought of being looked after, and fed, and of sleeping indoors overcame his fears. No longer would he have to beg or steal. And the food here was excellent.

"You must wash, Sam," said Mistress Giraud, interrupting his thoughts. "And I will find clean clothes..."

"Wait!" cried Sam.

He'd forgotten all about Budge!

"My dog..." he began, his voice shaking.

They all looked at Budge, who edged away from the cat and wagged his tail.

Husband and wife exchanged glances.

Master Giraud raised his eyebrows in enquiry.
Mistress Giraud shrugged her shoulders.

"He can stay," said Sam's new master.
And he smiled.

* * *

"You!" André glared at Sam. "You dare
to come here..."

They were in the back yard, where Sam
had washed first himself and then Budge,
and was now drying the dog with an old
cloth. Sam stood up. This was just what he
had feared.

He knew he was in the wrong. He'd been

cruel to this boy, mocking his lameness. He felt sorry, but it came out badly as he tried to excuse himself. "It was just a game – a laugh," he said.

"A laugh?" yelled André.

Budge was looking from one to the other of them, wagging his tail uncertainly. André patted him. "Pity we can't just keep the dog," he said.

"Well, you can't! He's mine!" Sam felt a sudden fear of losing everything. "Have you told your father what I did?"

"I don't tell tales," said André scornfully. "But remember: I belong here and you are just a pauper my mother felt sorry for. Any trouble from you, and they'll throw you out on the streets."

He turned his back on Sam and went indoors.

Sam couldn't blame André. He put his arms around Budge and the dog licked him.

"I must work hard and please Master and Mistress Giraud," he said. "We have a new home here, Budge. A new chance to make a life for ourselves. And we'll stay together, no matter what."